TIME TO SLEEP, LITTLE CRITTERS

BY MERCER MAYER

A Random House PICTUREBACK® Book

Random House 🏠 New York

Visit us on the Web! • rhcbooks.com • littlecritter.com

Educators and librarians, for a variety of teaching tools, visit us at RHTeachersLibrarians.com

ISBN 978-0-593-30202-6 (trade)

MANUFACTURED IN CHINA

10 9 8 7 6 5 4 3 2

JUST A NAP

BY
MERCER MAYER

Just when I was really having fun,
Mom said, "Time for a nap."

"But I'm not tired," I said.
"I won't be able to sleep."

Mom said, "Then close your eyes and just pretend to sleep."

Mom told me to lie down
on my special nap cot.
Then she pulled the shade.

"Not too dark," I said.

I tried to sleep. I even closed my eyes very tight.

But I just wasn't sleepy. I was thirsty.

So I got a drink.

Mom said, "Go take your nap and you won't be thirsty."

Then I was hungry, too, so I got some cookies.

But Mom took the cookies and said, "Cookies will taste even better after your nap."

"No, they won't," I said.
"They'll taste just the same."

"Trust me," said Mom, and
she took the cookies anyway.

I needed something to read to make
me sleepy. I got some comic books.

Mom took them, too. She said,
"No comics during naptime."

It was just too noisy to take a nap.

So Mom shut the bedroom window.
"Now you won't be disturbed," she said.

Then it was too quiet to sleep,
so I played a music tape.

Mom said, "The music will sound much better after a nap," and she took my tape player.

I got my teddy bear. He didn't want to take a nap either.

I told him a bedtime story
to make him sleepy.

We tried very hard
to take a nap . . .

. . . but we were just not sleepy at all.

JUST GO TO BED

BY
MERCER MAYER

I'm a cowboy and I round up cows.
I can lasso anything.

Dad says . . .

"It's time for the cowboy to come inside and get ready for bed."

I'm a general and I have to stop
the enemy army with my tank.

Dad says . . .

"It's time for the general to take a bath."

I'm a space cadet and I zoom to the moon.

I capture a robot with my ray gun.

Dad says . . .

I'm a sea monster attacking a ship.

Dad says, "It's time for the sea monster to have a snack."

I'm a zookeeper feeding my hungry animals.

Dad says . . .

"Feeding time is over. Here are the zookeeper's pajamas."

I'm Super Critter flying over the city.

I'm a train engineer being chased by bandits.

Dad says, "The bandit chief has caught you, so put on your pajamas."

But I'm a race car driver and I just speed away.

Dad says, "The race is over.
Now put on these pajamas
and go to bed."

I'm a bunny hopping
around my garden.

Dad says . . .

"Just go to bed!"

"But I'm a bunny and bunnies don't sleep in a bed."

Mom says, "Shhh!"
Dad says, "Go to sleep."

Well, maybe a tired
bunny could sleep in a
bed . . . just this once.